Don't Laugh at Giraffe

Rebecca Bender

pajamapress

First published in the United States in 2012
Text and illustrations copyright © 2012 Rebecca Bender
This edition copyright © 2012 Pajama Press

10 9 8 7 6 5 4 3 2 1

 Canada Council **Conseil des Arts**
for the Arts **du Canada**

 ONTARIO ARTS COUNCIL
CONSEIL DES ARTS DE L'ONTARIO

The publisher gratefully acknowledges the support of the Canada Council
for the Arts and the Ontario Arts Council for its publishing program. We
acknowledge the financial support of the Government of Canada through
the Canada Book Fund (CBF) for our publishing activities.

Library and Archives Canada Cataloguing in Publication

Bender, Rebecca
    Don't laugh at Giraffe / Rebecca Bender.

ISBN 978-0-9869495-6-2

    I. Title.

PS8603.E5562D66 2012   jC813'.6   C2012-901490-7

Publisher Cataloging-in-Publication Data (U.S.)

Bender, Rebecca, 1980-
    Don't laugh at giraffe / Rebecca Bender.
[ ] p. : col. ill. ;   cm.
Summary: Giraffe and Bird spat, squabble, and get on each other's nerves.
There's nothing the irrepressible Bird likes more than to have a laugh at the
expense of his dignified friend, and one thirsty day at the water hole, he gets
his chance. Giraffe's awkward attempt to reach the water without getting
his hooves wet raises a laugh from all his friends, even bird.   With giraffe's
feelings hurt, bird learn a lesson about hurting feelings and friendship.
ISBN-13: 978-0-9869495-6-2
1. Giraffe – Juvenile fiction. 1. Birds – Juvenile fiction. 1. Friendship –
Juvenile fiction. I. Title.
[E] dc23   PZ10.3B4634Do 2012

Manufactured by Friesens in Altona, Manitoba, Canada in March 2012.

Pajama Press Inc.
469 Richmond St E, Toronto Ontario, Canada
www.pajamapress.ca

The illustrations are painted with acrylic on texturized illustration board.

For Marc, who can always make me laugh

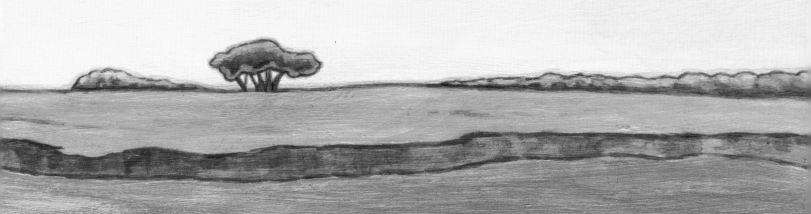

No one would argue that Giraffe and Bird
are an odd pair. Spat, scrap, and squabble—
they almost **always** get on each other's nerves.

The funny thing is,
you **rarely** see them apart.

Take this morning, for example.
The bird wakes up extra early and performs his **chirpiest** song.

Tweet-ta-
Loo- Loo- Loo-
Tweet-ta-
Loo- Loo-
Loo-

The sound of the bird chirping inspires the giraffe to clear his long **phlegmy** throat.

The sound of the giraffe clearing his throat sparks the bird to **flutter** around the giraffe's **sensitive** neck.

Hee

he

e hee hee

To escape the flurry of fluttering
the ticklish giraffe breaks into a trot.

When the bird sees the giraffe trot,
he can't help but race after him.

When the giraffe senses the bird swoop after him,
he scrambles to go faster than his legs will allow.

It doesn't take long before...

... all that hurrying leaves them both very thirsty.

At the pond the water is much lower than usual.

The bird **doesn't** notice. He **tosses** the water in the air and enjoys a refreshing drink.

The giraffe **does** notice.
He **stands** at the water's edge
and tries to figure out a way to quench his thirst
without getting his hooves wet.

First, the giraffe reaches down and **stretches out** his **flexible** tongue as far as he can.

AH- CLACK
CLACK

This gets him a cackle
from the flamingo,
but no water.

Next, he extends his neck,
stretches out his tongue,
and **squats** down
as low as he can.

This gathers a **howl** from the hippo,
some **cheeps** from the bird,
but still no water.

Oh-Hoo-Hoo

cheep
cheep
Chirrup

Last, he sticks out his tail for balance,
extends his neck, and does the **splits**.
Finally he can feel water
on the tip of his tongue!

That's when the zebra joins in...

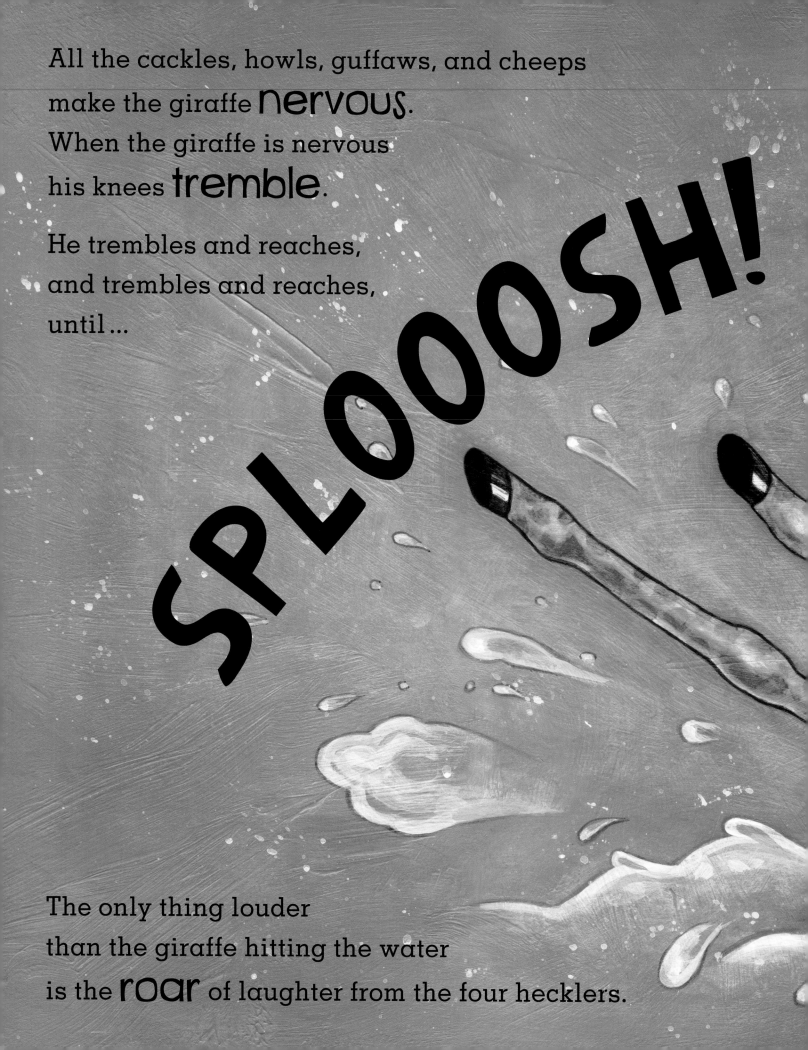

All the cackles, howls, guffaws, and cheeps
make the giraffe nervous.
When the giraffe is nervous
his knees tremble.

He trembles and reaches,
and trembles and reaches,
until...

SPLOOOOSH!

The only thing louder
than the giraffe hitting the water
is the roar of laughter from the four hecklers.

No one but the bird notices the giraffe slink away,
still thirsty, but too **embarrassed** to stick around.

The giraffe finds a nearby puddle.
His ears are **droopy**,
his eyes are **misty**,
and his nose is **sniffly**
as he laps at the muddy water.

Sniff
Sniff

The bird is sorry
to see the giraffe so unhappy.
He has some thinking to do.

How can he make things right?

Luckily, the bird comes up with his best ideas under pressure.

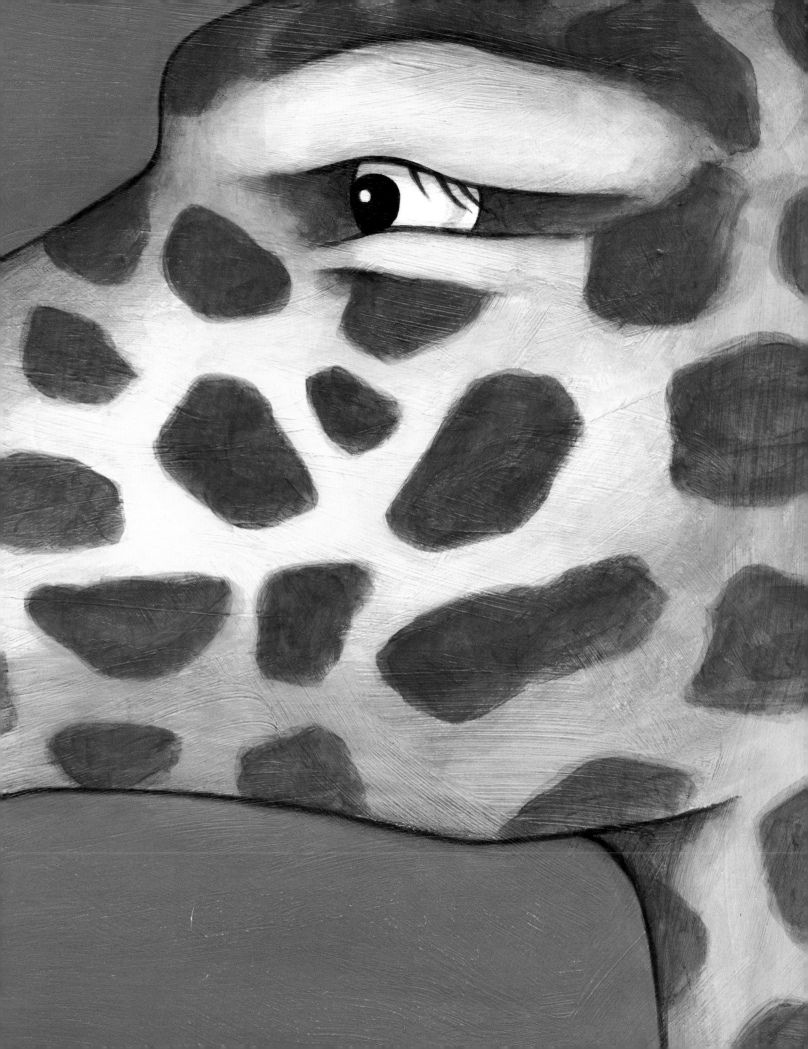

Back at the pond,
the zebra spots the giraffe first.

HEE-YA

HE

AW
E-YAAW

Well, that's all it takes for
the giraffe's knees to **tremble**.
Just when he is about to
slink away again,
out **pops** the bird...

Oh-Hoo-Hoo

Tweet~ta~ Loo-Loo

Tweet~ta~ Loo-Loo

Hhyuck Hhyuck

Everyone laughs.
Even the giraffe laughs.
The **silly-looking** bird makes
the giraffe feel better
about **looking silly.**

Anyone can see that the bird loves the attention,

but at least everyone has a laugh...

...and the giraffe finally has a drink.

Best of all,
the giraffe isn't afraid
to get his hooves wet
anymore.